P9-APO-702

To my parents who love and support me without reward

Originally published by Sang Publishing, Seoul, Korea, as *Grimmie's White Canvas*
English translation by Mi-Kyoung Chang.

First English edition 2015

Published by Peter Pauper Press, Inc.
202 Mamaroneck Avenue
White Plains, New York 10601
U.S.A.

Designed by Heather Zschock

Library of Congress Cataloging-in-Publication Data Available

ISBN 978-1-4413-1826-8
Manufactured for Peter Pauper Press, Inc.
Printed in Hong Kong

7 6 5 4 3 2 1

Visit us at www.peterpauper.com

Mina's White Canvas

HYEON-JU LEE

It was a gray and gloomy day outside.
And when Mina looked up at the winter sky,
it made her feel gray and gloomy too.

So she took her crayon and
began to draw white snowflakes
in the gray sky.

Every time Mina drew one snowflake,
more and more fell onto the ground.

And before she knew it,
the whole world was covered in snow.
Mina decided to explore.

"Hello!" she shouted.
"Is anyone there?"
Her voice filled up the quiet forest.

Then she heard a voice nearby.

"Hello!" it said. "Up here!"

She peeked through ice-covered branches and followed the voice up to the top of a tree.

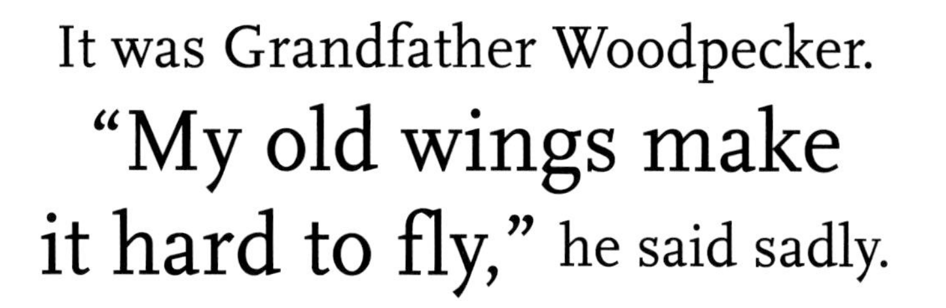

It was Grandfather Woodpecker.
"My old wings make
it hard to fly," he said sadly.

Mina took out her crayon and drew a ladder.
With each rung, she climbed
higher and higher.

"What a wonderful ladder!"
said Grandfather Woodpecker as Mina
helped him down to the ground.

The new friends walked through the forest.

"Look!" said Mina.
"I see someone in that cave!"

It was Mr. Bear. He had grown so fat during the long winter that he was stuck in the cave opening.

Mina and Grandfather Woodpecker pulled and tugged, but they could not get him out.

Mina took her crayon and drew a big
blue door on the side of the cave.

Hooray! It was just the right size for Mr. Bear!

Overjoyed to be free, Mr. Bear ran out into the snow.

"Let's slide down the hill!"

he yelled to his new friends.

Whooaaahhh! They slid down the hill so fast that they landed at the bottom, near a lake, with a big THUD.

The sound was so loud that it woke up Miss Frog,
who poked her head out of the snow-covered
lake to see what the big fuss was.

"Hello!" said Mina. "Do you want to come out and play with us?"

"I'd love to," replied Miss Frog, "but I have no fur, feathers, or clothes. I would be too cold!"

Mina knew just what to do. She pulled out her crayon and drew warm, fuzzy red socks for Miss Frog's feet. They fit perfectly!

Miss Frog was so excited that she began hopping all around in the snow.

Hippity-Hop! Hippity-Hop! Hippity-Hop!

Mina, Grandfather Woodpecker, and Mr. Bear joined in the fun!

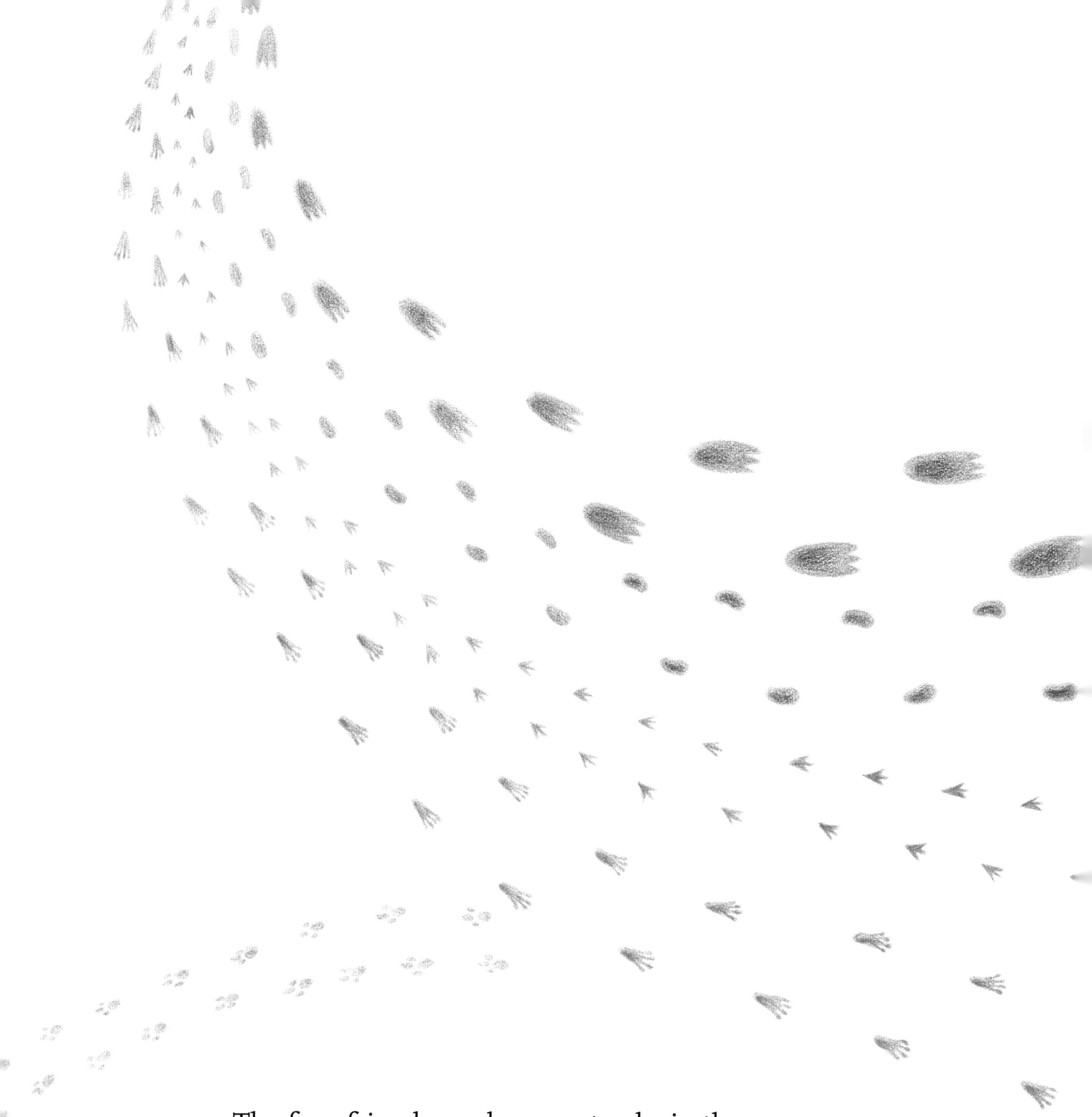

The four friends made many tracks in the snow.
But Mina noticed something strange.

“Look!” she said.
“Whose footprints are those?”

They followed the footprints through the snow.
Soon they came upon Baby Bunny, who was crying.

"What's wrong?" Mina asked.

"I lost my mommy," sobbed Baby Bunny.
"My fur is as white as snow,
and she won't ever be able to find
me in this snowy field."

Mina had an idea. She pointed
to Baby Bunny's footprints and said,
"Let's follow them backward from here."

Everyone agreed that was a good idea.

Together, side by side, they followed
the path of footprints . . .

. . . which led Baby Bunny
right to Mama Bunny,

who gave him a big hug!

Mina's crayon was wearing out,
but she decided to use it one more time.

She wanted to make sure Baby and Mama Bunny
would never lose each other again.

It was now late in the day and
time for Mina to go home.

Her friends waved good-bye.
"Let's play again soon!"
they said.

As the sun set in the forest, Mina looked back again and again, waving until she couldn't see her friends anymore.

Mina's crayon had worn away,
but her memories of the wonderful winter day
were as bright as the colors in her heart.